THE EVERYTHING KIDS' DRAGONS

PUZZLE AND ACTIVITY BOOK

From scales to tails, fire-breathing
excitement every kid will love

Scot Ritchie

A adamsmedia

Avon, Massachusetts

PUBLISHER Karen Cooper

DIRECTOR OF ACQUISITIONS AND INNOVATION Paula Munier

MANAGING EDITOR, EVERYTHING SERIES Lisa Laing

COPY CHIEF Casey Ebert

ACQUISITIONS EDITOR Katie McDonogh

DEVELOPMENT EDITOR Elizabeth Kassab

EDITORIAL ASSISTANT Hillary Thompson

An Everything® Series Book.
Everything® and everything.com® are registered trademarks of F+W Publications, Inc.

Published by Adams Media, an F+W Publications Company
57 Littlefield Street, Avon, MA 02322. U.S.A.
www.adamsmedia.com

ISBN-10: 1-59869-623-8
ISBN-13: 978-1-59869-623-3

Printed in the United States of America.

J I H G F E D C B A

This publication is designed to provide accurate and authoritative information with regard to
the subject matter covered. It is sold with the understanding that the publisher is not engaged
in rendering legal, accounting, or other professional advice. If legal advice or other expert
assistance is required, the services of a competent professional person should be sought.
—From a *Declaration of Principles* jointly adopted by a Committee of the
American Bar Association and a Committee of Publishers and Associations

Many of the designations used by manufacturers and sellers to distinguish their products are
claimed as trademarks. When those designations appear in this book and Adams Media was
aware of a trademark claim, the designations have been printed with initial capital letters.

Cover illustrations by Dana Regan.
Interior illustrations by Kurt Dolber.
Puzzles by Scot Ritchie.

This book is available at quantity discounts for bulk purchases.
For information, please call 1-800-289-0963.

CONTENTS

INTRODUCTION

Dragons are found throughout history dating back thousands of years. There are stories from Greece, Germany, England, Norway, Japan, China, Indonesia, and more. It's almost enough to make you think they really existed. We have no proof (like bones or fossils), but at one time explorers really did believe they existed. They came back from their world travels with stories of dragon graves and monsters at sea. If you look at ancient maps you will often see dragons on the borders. This was a way of showing places too dangerous to explore. Often what the explorers really saw were crocodiles or elephants. But those were animals they had never seen before so it is easy to see how they could make a mistake. If you stumbled on a large snake or a Komodo dragon on a dark, stormy night you could very well believe it was a magic dragon.

The word *dragon* comes from the Latin word *draco*. This word has different meanings. The one used for dragons means a constellation of stars in the northern sky. I bet if you look at the stars at night you could find some dragons up there.

Dragons were considered to be one of the scariest beasts ever. They had long, sharp talons, big razorlike teeth, and a lot of them could fly. And if that's not enough, they could also breathe fire. That's enough to make most people sit up and take notice—or run away screaming. When someone can shoot flames out of their mouth, it's always a good idea to stay away.

Which brings us to our next point: They were very solitary creatures. Now we can see why!

To Europeans, dragons were nasty, dirty creatures. They liked to live in dark, wet caverns with the remains of their dinners scattered around. Imagine the smell. Peeyewww!

In Asia they were very different. They were civilized and clean. Most dragons lived in the sky or in oceans or rivers. As you can imagine, dragons were much more popular with Asians. In fact, they were seen as signs of luck or bravery.

Dragons came in all shapes and sizes, from super-giant to pip-squeak. In Russia some dragons were so big their wings would darken the sky as they flew overhead. In Japan some were so tiny they could fit inside a raindrop.

Sometimes they would hang out with each other (well, no one else would!), but usually that didn't last too long. They would start boasting how far they could shoot flames and get into fire-breathing contests. The next thing you know, there goes another village! You can see why people didn't want them in the neighborhood.

Dragons really seemed to have a thing for royalty—either eating them or stealing their jewels. A lot of dragon stories involve a brave knight riding in to rescue a princess. If he was successful he would get her hand in marriage. If he wasn't, let's just say he was one crispy knight. Some modern stories have turned things around and the girl rides in to rescue the boy (because girls are just as brave as boys, it just depends what they're up against).

Dragons have provided us with great stories and adventures, so we should really thank them for that. And it seems that in modern times they are keeping their distance, so we should thank them for that too!

So if you're feeling brave, grab your shield and pen and let's go find some dragons!

The Horrible Hydra

The Hydra was a terrifying many-headed monster. He had anywhere from five to over 100 heads. His job was to guard the entrance to the Underworld (the place where dead souls would go). Can you finish off these faces? We've done one to get you started. What do you think he looked like?

What do you say when you meet a five-headed dragon?

Hello, hello, hello, hello, hello!

St. George the Gentleman

Once upon a time, a dragon was terrorizing the people of a small town. St. George heard that the villagers were ready to offer a princess to the dragon in exchange for sparing their town. St. George was a very nice person and didn't think that was very fair so he rode into town and killed the dragon. This wonderful story has been around for centuries. The only problem is it took place in the twelfth century, long after St. George had died.

Can you help George through the maze to save the town?

SHADOW DRAGON
It looks like the shadows of some of these dragons aren't quite right. Can you pick the one that is correct?

What sound do fire-breathing dragons make when they kiss?

Ouch!

Ring of the Nibelung

Dragons have appeared in movies, stories, and operas. There's even an opera called the *Ring of the Nibelung* that features a dragon called Fafnir. He was the son of the dwarf king, Hreidmar. Fafnir turned himself into a fearsome dragon when he realized it was the only way to get some gold that had been left to his brother. Now you can see why dragons have such a bad reputation!

Tail in Mouth

In Norse mythology, Jormungand is a monster so dangerous that he was thrown into the sea to protect humankind. This is one HUGE dragon—he circles the entire earth and can put his tail in his mouth. When the universe is destroyed, Jormungand and Thor (the god of thunder) will kill each other. That's going to be one noisy battle!

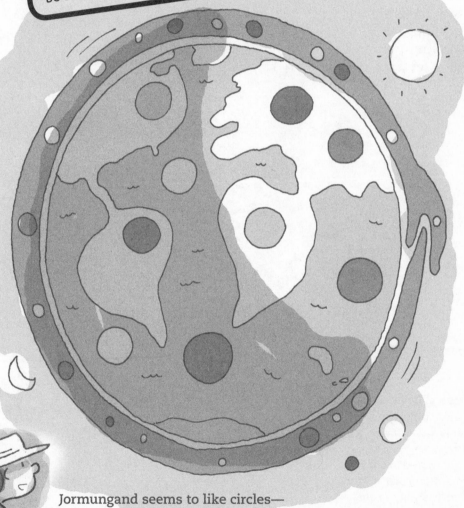

Jormungand seems to like circles—how many can you count here?

Elephants for Dinner

In Ethiopia it is said that giant dragons lived in the ocean and came ashore to hunt elephants. Only when their food supply began to dwindle did the dragons move on to other hunting grounds. And they did it in style—four or five of them would twist together like rope, lift their heads out of the water, and set off for new lands.

These dragons are mixing things up and causing quite a mess. Can you see six things that don't belong?

Unlucky Dragon
Dracontias is the name of a stone that comes from the brain of a dragon. It is believed to bring health and prosperity. The only catch is you can only get it from a living dragon.

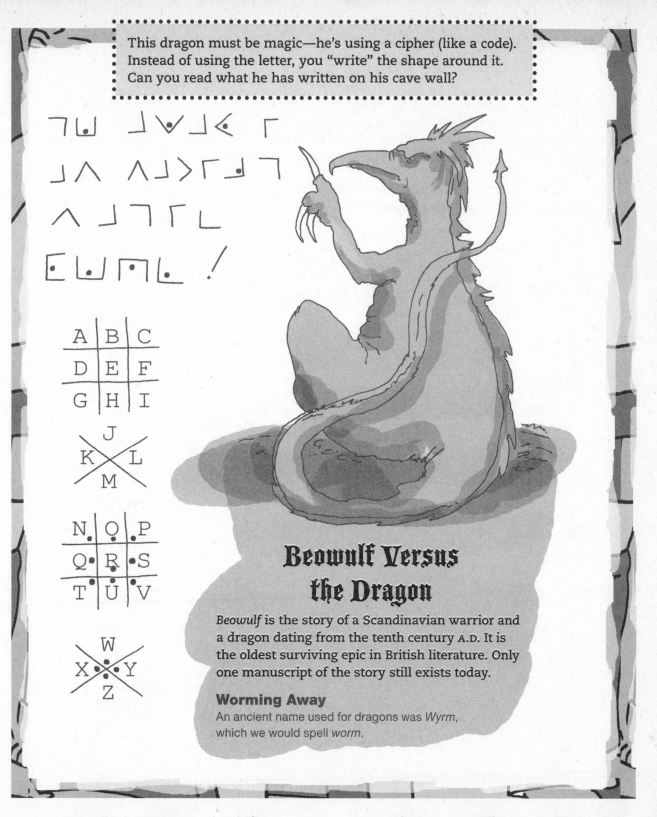

Beowulf Versus the Dragon

Beowulf is the story of a Scandinavian warrior and a dragon dating from the tenth century A.D. It is the oldest surviving epic in British literature. Only one manuscript of the story still exists today.

Worming Away

An ancient name used for dragons was *Wyrm*, which we would spell *worm*.

Smaug

Smaug was the name of the dragon in J. R. R. Tolkien's book *The Hobbit*. Like a lot of dragons, he liked to hoard jewels. His stomach was covered with gems, which made him very difficult to kill (most dragons' only vulnerable spot was their belly). But he did have one spot that was unprotected. Can you figure out where it is by breaking this code?

The World Tree

Nidhogg, or "tearer of corpses," was a dragon from ancient Norse mythology. When he wasn't eating corpses he would gnaw at the roots of the World Tree—a tree that was said to link and shelter all the parts of the world. Without roots a tree wouldn't stand. Besides "roots," there are some other words with two Os in them that are very useful.

Set Down Roots
You can grow plants at home with just a bowl of water. It's best if you use a glass container. Some of the best plants to grow are the umbrella plant, Chinese evergreen, arrowhead plant, and grape ivy.

A roof is on top of the house.

If you cut yourself you see Blood

We need to eat food to survive.

When you look in the night sky you can see the Moon

If a dragon is attacking, shoot your arrow at him!

To sweep his cave a dragon needs a good Broom.

The Groom kissed the bride.

When you eat soup a Spoon is helpful.

A big motorbike goes Vroom

Dragons are featured in some _ _ _ _ oo _ _ .

Terrified Townsfolk

These townsfolk were so brave they banded together and tried to kill the dragon that was terrorizing their town. Before they could celebrate, they learned this dragon was able to join its body together again and carry on as if nothing had happened! Can you put these pieces back together and see what it looked like?

What do you do when a dragon sneezes?

Get out of the way!

Too Many Heads

This three-headed dragon is guarding the entrance to the evil king's palace. Can you help the brave (but confused) knight find his way through?

The study of dragon lore is called *draconology*.

exit

enter

Careful Counting

People born in the year of the dragon are said to be lively, powerful, and lucky. The year 2000 was a year of the dragon. How many 2000s can you see on this dragon?

12 animals

There are twelve animals in Chinese astrology:
rat, tiger, dragon, horse, monkey, dog, ox, rabbit, snake, sheep, rooster, and pig.

Mississippi Mane

There was a dragon that lived near the Mississippi River in North America. After years of terrorizing the Illini tribe, the tribe members banded together and followed his giant tracks back to his cave. Armed with weapons, they lured the dragon outside and killed him. Look at the footprints left behind by this giant dragon—they're huge! But something is wrong with this picture. Can you see which track just doesn't belong?

Horrific Heraldic

The Heraldic Dragon was one of the most fearsome with its barbed tail, spiked nose, and dangerous spines on its back. It was said you could tell the age of some dragons by the number of spines. How old is this dragon?

Each spine represents 10 years.

Stormy Sayings

On November 30 in the year 1222, dragons were seen flying over the city of London. Some people believed they caused the thunderstorm and severe flooding that followed. This dragon looks like he's trying to help. Can you make out what the clouds say? Be careful—the wind has blown the letters around so they will need to be put back in their proper order.

Knock Knock Who's there? Dragon! Dragon who? Dragon your feet again!

Ancient Courage

Dragons are feared in the West, but in China they symbolized courage and heroism. They were believed to be a combination of nine animals: deer (horns), camel (head), devil (eyes), snake (neck), cockle (abdomen), carp (scales), eagle (claws), tiger (paws), and ox (ears).

IMAGINANIMAL

There are five animals squished together in this imaginary creature. Can you match the name with the body part?

DUCK

EAGLE

HORSE

FISH

BULL

Norse Numbers

Most often these fire-breathing creatures liked to live alone, but this cave is full of dragons. How many can you find?

What time is it when you see a dragon in the kitchen making breakfast with your mom's dress on?

Time to wake up and go to school!

Greek Guard Dog

In ancient Greece, dragons were often used to guard entrances. Most people would think twice about trying to get past this dragon. It looks like he's been taking a few things as well as guarding the door. Can you find all these things he's collected in his cave?

1 each: shovel, bouquet of flowers, belt
2 each: feathers, skulls, mirrors, purses
3 each: shields, helmets, swords
4 each: balls, gloves, spoons, shirts, scarves

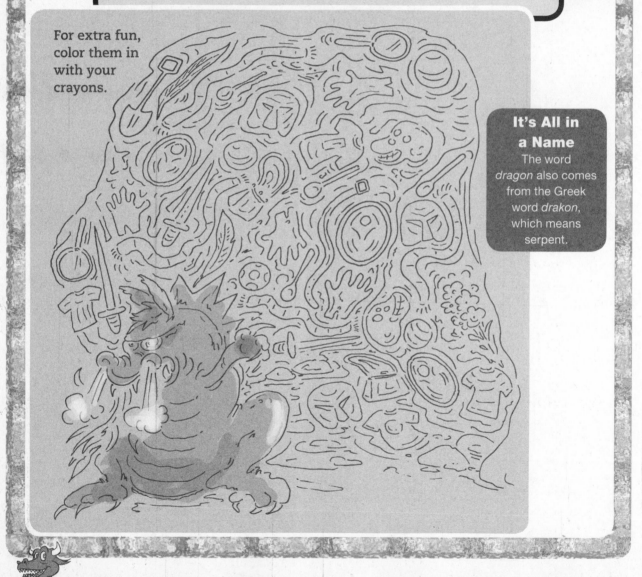

For extra fun, color them in with your crayons.

It's All in a Name
The word *dragon* also comes from the Greek word *drakon*, which means serpent.

Horse and All

Ancient Persia (what is now Iran) had its fair share of vicious and hungry dragons. One story tells of a king by the name of Ardashir riding through the mountains of Persia when he (and his horse!) were swallowed whole. The dragon was so fast the king didn't have time to turn and escape.

Here's a fun game. How fast are you? Try to figure out these matching words—they mean different things but they sound the same—like *name* and *game*.

A dance in
the autumn:

_____

What the ruler
wears on his finger:

_____

A big boat:

_____

Colorful sticky stuff:

_____

Cherokee Crystal

The Cherokee people of North America had their own monster, called the Uk'ten, who could breathe fire and fly. What made him unique was that he had antlers and a giant crystal in his forehead. He could kill with a look and speak in the language of the people around him. What language is this dragon speaking? Here's a tip: move one letter in each word and it all becomes clear.

Od otn ngera em ro oury illageu illw eb estroyedd!

All for One

Dragons from Byzantine times were often shown eating their own tail with the phrase "the all is one." The meaning was similar to the Chinese yin and yang. It represents the idea of balance. One of these dragons isn't as balanced as he should be. Can you see which one has an even number of white stripes and an uneven number of white dots?

INSIDE DRAGON
What do these words all have in common? grand, road, grad, nod, and groan

Rockin' Russia

Alicha was one of the scariest dragons in Russia. It was believed his black wings could cover the sky. The story goes that he tried to eat the moon and sun but failed. All that remained were his teeth marks, which we see as the dark markings on the moon today. People in Russia would throw rocks at an eclipse to make Alicha go away.

ORAAKHILA

KLLAHA

CLAHIHA

IAHCLA

RAAKHO

OHKORAA

CLALIHA

HAAKLLA

ALKLHA AND ARAKHO

These are the other names Alicha was known by. Whatever he was called, these villagers just want to get away, but the only escape is to follow a path with the correct spelling of the three names. There is one correct path for each name.

21

Mexican Monster

There is one type of dragon that has no arms or legs—just wings and fearsome teeth. The most famous example is the Quetzalcoatl. Because there is a bird found in Mexico called the Quetzal, many people believe this is where the dragon got its name. Both have bright green feathers and shimmer as they fly.

This dragon has collected a lot of coins.

Which coin appears most often? _____

Which coin only appears once? _____

How many different coins can you see? _____

How many are heads? _____

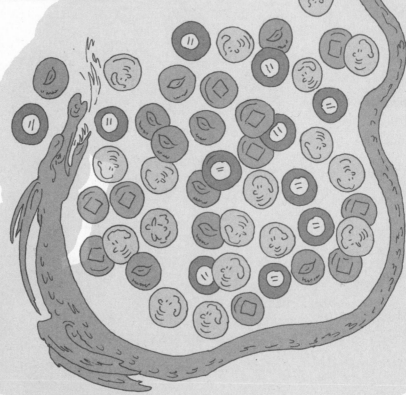

Dragon eggs are usually the same color as the mother dragon.

Come on, Komodo!

Indonesia is the only place in the world where we can still see real dragons. They don't breathe fire or fly, but they do have razor-sharp teeth. They are able to swallow a meal up to 80 percent of their own size. Their ancestors were living on the island of Komodo about 50 million years ago.

KOMODOKOMODO

How many times can you see the word *Komodo* written here? You can read it forwards, backwards, up, and down but not diagonally.

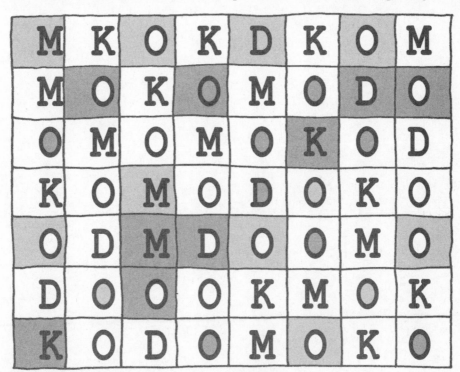

M	K	O	K	D	K	O	M
M	O	K	O	M	O	D	O
O	M	O	M	O	K	O	D
K	O	M	O	D	O	K	O
O	D	M	D	O	O	M	O
D	O	O	K	M	O	K	
K	O	D	O	M	O	K	O

Dragondiddle Riddle
What is just as big as a dragon but weighs nothing at all?

His shadow.

Dragon Digits

Dragons have a very long history in Japan, and they are still very active in modern times. They are featured in everything from anime series to movies to video games. One way to recognize a Japanese dragon from other dragons is they always have three claws instead of four. Some have wings and some don't. How many Japanese dragons can you count here?

Nine Lives

In Japan some people believed that dragons gave birth to nine babies, each with a different attribute like being a singer or being lazy or brave.

DRAW A NAGA
What would this dragon look like if you gave it a human face?

Naga Dragon

The dragons of India were known as the Naga. They were often shown with the face of a human. In fact, they could change their whole body to appear as a human. They were treated with great respect because they controlled the weather and could cause flooding or droughts if angered.

Why did the dragon eat a person?

Because he wanted to become more personable.

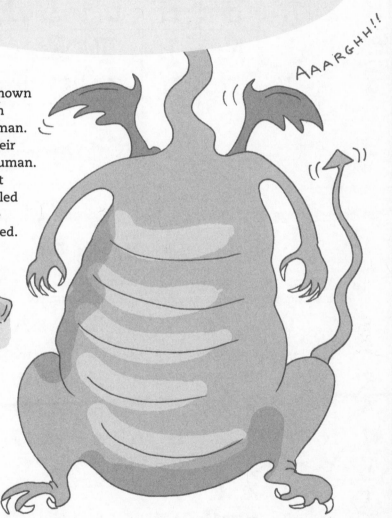

AAARGHH!!

In Africa the dragons are huge. It was said their twisting and turning created the valleys and rivers. Their dung created the mountains and hills. Some were so big they were mistaken for mountains. Remove every S, F, and L to reveal a message left by the dragon.

Writhing Rivers

S	I	L	F	L	M	F	S
A	F	D	F	E	L	S	T
L	H	E	L	L	M	O	F
U	N	L	T	F	F	A	I
L	L	N	S	F	F	S	S

Abraxas to Zu

Abraxas was a dragon from Persian mythology and Zu was the symbol of chaos from Sumerian mythology. To find the name of another famous dragon:

E	T	L	L	M	P	S	E	A	A	U
B	F	G	C	E	E	D	G	H	R	J
K	Q	T	U	T	V	A	M	W	W	Y
A	C	W	X	X	I	D	E	H	H	U
W	N	F	E	E	H	A	A	M	Q	T
V	V	W	B	Z	Z	M	H	H	S	E
T	T	O	K	K	T	E	F	B	A	A
C	D	G	H	W	W	J	P	K	L	M

Remove any letter that is not one of these:

N, O, I, B, P, R, or S

Princess Pal

This dragon has made friends with the princess instead of eating her, and she's very happy about that. They love to collect shells on the beach together. The shells all look alike, but only two are an exact match. Can you find them?

Why did the dragon paint his talons different colors?

So he could hide in the jellybeans.

28

Watch Out, Wizard!

This wizard knows where everything is in his cave. But he's having a bad day today and has mixed up his spells. There are ten changes in these two scenes. Can you spot them?

Which Witch?

This witch was casting a spell, but the dragon got in and tore up the paper. Can you put the pieces back together to see what it said?

my words,
If you
will follow
Trouble and

dragon will
and fire YOU!

don't heed
Druid the
fly over

and
and
toil!
bubble
YOU!

Heave
weave
spoil and

Patient: Doctor, I keep seeing dragons with purple spots!

Doctor: Hmmm, have you seen an eye doctor?

Meet the Mermaid

Some stories tell of dragons and mermaids meeting. These two share a cave, and they both love gemstones and shiny things. Can you unscramble the letters to see what this dragon has hoarded? Then unscramble the circled letters to see his favorite shiny thing.

byru _ _ _ _

amddisno _ _ _ _ _ _ _ _

ranteg _ _ _ _ _ _

mareeld _ _ _ _ _ _ _

pphaires _ _ _ _ _ _ _ _

sythemat _ _ _ _ _ _ _ _

realp _ _ _ _ _

Circle Game
Why did the dragon keep turning around in a circle?

He wanted to read a long tail.

Day and Knight

It seemed like knights were doing battle with dragons every day. Considering the size difference, it's a good thing knights had armor to protect themselves. Can you see how you would travel through this knight's armor to the top?

finish

start

Scale Tale

Most dragons have protection too, and it grows right on them! They're called scales—just like you would find on a fish but much tougher.

Fake Fairies

Many people who believed in dragons
also believed in fairies. In the early 1900s,
some people took photographs of
what they said were real fairies dancing
in the garden. Arthur Conan Doyle
(who wrote all the Sherlock Holmes books)
believed in fairies so much, he even wrote
his own book about them. These fairies
all look very similar but only two are
exactly alike—can you find them?

**What did the
grape do when the
dragon sat on it?**

**It gave out
a little
wine.**

Gggriffins

Like dragons, griffins were pretty nasty monsters. People would look up in surprise to see a griffin grimacing down at them. They could sure scare you late at night!

To find out where griffins like to hang out, fill in every letter that isn't a T, P, R, O, F, or S.

B	L	E	R	E
D	O	L	A	D
D	M	C	O	L
C	L	E	B	E
A	F	B	C	M
L	E	C	T	B
C	O	D	A	D
M	A	E	M	P
S	C	B	D	L

Bird's-Eye View

Can you connect the dots and see where this bird is going to land?

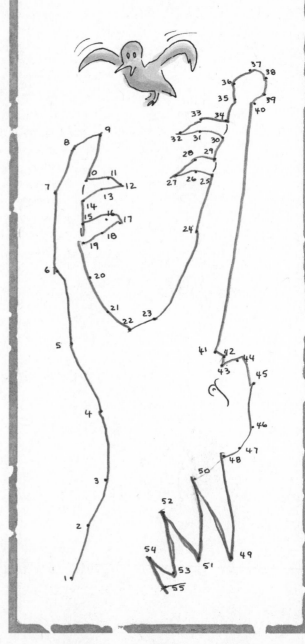

H S S N O M E A K
C C J K E Q U Q A
A E W C L K N O R
W I O Y E O O U G
S E T S Y I O U R
D J W E W S E L R
S F B Q A C N K O

King's Ransom

This dragon has stolen all kinds of jewels from the king. But the king has some magic of his own. All he has to do is read the dark gems and ignore the light ones to uncover the magic phrase and get his jewels back. Can you help him?

Flying Fire

This dragon looks he's trying to be one of the flock.
Which one doesn't fit in?

36

Adapt a Dragon

In Asia, dragons could turn into water-dwelling creatures. Can you see what these turn into? Figure out the clue, then drop the first letter for a new word.

Drop the first letter from a  and you get a group of people who play the same sport.

Drop the first letter from a and you get a long distance.

Drop the first letter from a and you get a kind of wood.

Drop the first letter from a and you get someone who can do things well.

Drop the first letter from a and you get the thing you put on your bike so it's safe.

Hand to Head

Dragons get cold in the winter just like you do. Dirk the dragon has six pairs of mittens and five hats. How many different combinations can Dirk wear?

Unicorn or Not

Just like dragons, unicorns were thought to be real by many people. The early Greeks believed they lived in India. Can you tell which one of these is a real unicorn? Hint: Real unicorns have four main features: horn, cloven hooves, lion's tail, and beard.

Horn of the Unicorn

In medieval times, people who feared they had been poisoned would search for a goblet made of unicorn horn. It was believed to neutralize poisons.

Straight from the Egg

Dragon moms and dads have just as much fun picking a name for their baby dragonets as we do for our babies. Can you figure out what first letter goes with what name?

It's All in a Name
One of the characters in the Harry Potter books is named Draco. Do you know his last name?

A B C D E F G H I J K L M N O P Q R S T U V W X Y Z

_asey	_essica	_annah	_ictoria
_orman	_eon	_im	_endy
_red	_eckham	_oris	_sadora
_erry	_atthew	_onny	_asmin
_iver	_rville	_anadu	_laine
_ephyr	_etra	_ravis	
_lan	_ueenie	_ma	

Goo Goo

These twin baby dragons look exactly the same, but there are actually ten differences. Can you spot them?

On a Scale of 1 to 10

You can tell the health of a dragon by looking at his scales. If he's feeling good they are bright and shiny. But if he's feeling ill they are dull and the color is grayish.

First Steps

When a baby dragon is learning to talk, Mom has to speak in code. Can you figure out what she's saying?

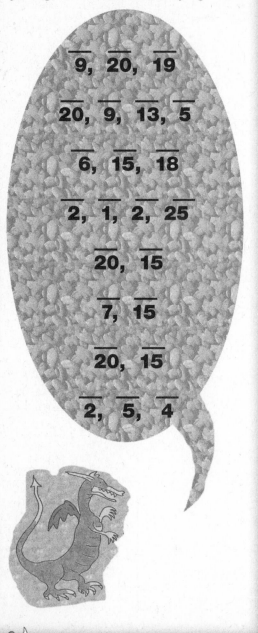

$\overline{9,}$ $\overline{20,}$ $\overline{19}$

$\overline{20,}$ $\overline{9,}$ $\overline{13,}$ $\overline{5}$

$\overline{6,}$ $\overline{15,}$ $\overline{18}$

$\overline{2,}$ $\overline{1,}$ $\overline{2,}$ $\overline{25}$

$\overline{20,}$ $\overline{15}$

$\overline{7,}$ $\overline{15}$

$\overline{20,}$ $\overline{15}$

$\overline{2,}$ $\overline{5,}$ $\overline{4}$

Careful, Baby!

What's the coolest trick a dragon can do? Breathe fire, of course! It looks like this dragon has already done some damage. How many "fires" can you see here?

Alphadragon

This dragon is off to school, and on the way he's trying to learn his alphabet. Can you see something that starts with every letter from A to Z?

Fly Way

Dragon wings can be any size. In fact, some Asian dragons are able to fly without any wings at all. They use their magic powers to get them off the ground.

   43

Teenage Trouble

Here's a teenage dragon with a sweet tooth playing tricks on the villagers. Can you see what he's written?*

*Here's a clue: Read every second letter starting with the I on the left. When you get to the end, turn around and read back up to the front.

E I T W A I L L O L C S O A H V C E
E Y M O G U N R I V R I B L U L O A
Y G F E I

Dragon Cake

Do you like cake? Ask your mom if you can help decorate a cake just like your favorite dragon! Go online to see all kinds of crazy ideas for making dragon-shaped cakes.

Young Love

This teenage dragon is checking herself out in the mirror. She's got a big date and wants to look nice. It looks like she's trying out a few different faces. Can you tell which emotion goes with which face?

SURPRISED · SLEEPY · SAD

CONFUSED · ANGRY

Why did the dragon cross the road?

To eat the chicken on the other side!

Dragon Wings

Some dragons can fly, so they get to see a lot of the world. This dragon is trying to land, but she can only land on islands where the total is an odd number. Can you help her?

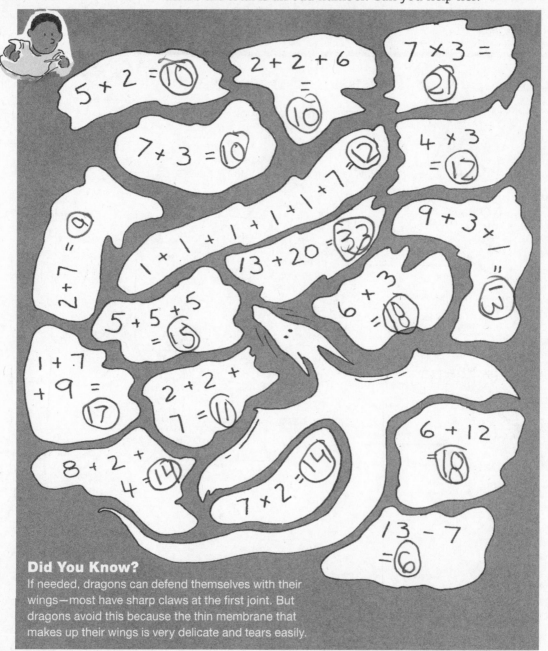

$5 \times 2 = 10$

$2 + 2 + 6 = 10$

$7 \times 3 = 21$

$7 + 3 = 10$

$1 + 1 + 1 + 1 + 7 = 12$

$4 \times 3 = 12$

$2 + 7 = 9$

$13 + 20 = 33$

$9 + 3 \times 1 = 13$

$6 \times 3 = 18$

$5 + 5 + 5 = 15$

$1 + 7 + 9 = 17$

$2 + 2 + 7 = 11$

$8 + 2 + 4 = 14$

$7 \times 2 = 14$

$6 + 12 = 18$

$13 - 7 = 6$

Did You Know?
If needed, dragons can defend themselves with their wings—most have sharp claws at the first joint. But dragons avoid this because the thin membrane that makes up their wings is very delicate and tears easily.

Drawing Dragons

Here's a close-up view of a dragon's feet, but he's lost almost all his scales. Can you help protect him again? Grab your pencils and crayons and get drawing!

Full-Scale Protection

One reason dragons could live for hundreds of years was that they were covered with a protective layer of scales—just like armor. But there was one vulnerable spot on their body that wasn't covered. Do you know where it was?

It's in the Stars

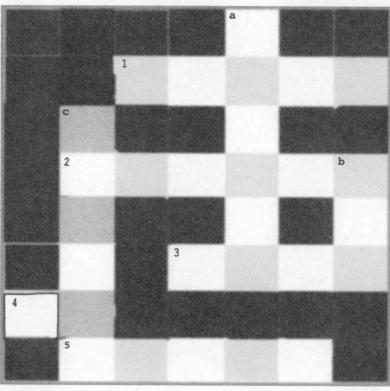

If your birthday is between April 5 and May 4, you are born under the sign of the dragon in the Chinese zodiac, and you like to do things on a grand scale and have a natural charm. People in this sign grow up to be kings, politicians, athletes, and explorers. Here are some more words that describe the dragon.

ACROSS

1. Very fortunate

2. Creative type

3. To lend a hand

4. Not off but . . .

5. Really, really good

DOWN

A. Very lively

B. Not the bottom but the . . .

C. Someone who looks after someone is a . . .

Go Dragon, Go!

Dragons were always on the go, and that makes sense since you can find the word *go* in their name. Here's some other words that have the letters GO in them. Can you see what they are?

Not badness but
GO_ _ _ _ _ _

GO_ _ _ _ _ _ _ _
and the three bears

A boy's name:
GO_ _ _ _

This bird honks:
GO_ _ _

The great
GO_ _
rush

Dark blue is known as
_ _ _ _GO

If you are going to the ball you wear a GO_ _

The Disney dog with big ears:
GO_ _ _

Crazy Crowns

This little dragon is having a birthday. Dragons love jewels and gold. Even though it's already wrapped, can you see which crown he's getting?

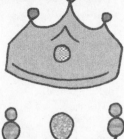

Just a Greedy Monster

European dragons are thought of as greedy and evil. Some stuffed their caves full of jewelry and every kind of gem.

50

Dragon Detective

Dragons aren't always out burning villages and scaring peasants. Sometimes they like to go to a friend's place and play games. In this game you will find five groups of objects in the sand, each divided into quarters. Can you see which one doesn't belong?

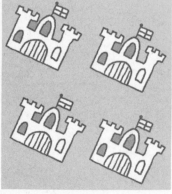

Yard Work

What do you get when you cross a dragon with a mole?

A giant hole in your garden.

Your Indoor Voice

If dragons want to make friends, they have to keep their voices down. (They usually just roar!) Can you help them find the "please" and the "thank you" in these letters? There is one of each.

L	O	O	U	P	L	E	O	S	E
Y	U	O	T	P	E	P	L	Y	K
U	P	N	E	E	S	E	N	O	Y
U	O	P	L	E	A	S	E	Y	B
B	P	P	L	E	S	T	Y	T	Y
N	L	T	T	G	G	S	U	S	H
O	E	H	T	J	I	O	T	S	Y
S	A	O	E	A	P	R	G	R	H
H	O	G	F	G	I	R	E	F	T
T	H	A	N	K	Y	O	U	S	G
Y	O	Y	T	H	A	A	S	E	R
U	U	U	K	Y	S	A	S	E	F

ARRRRooaaarrr!
Here's a fun game—see if you can make yourself understood to your friends without using any words. All you can do is roar, but you can make faces and use your hands.

Dragon Spell

This dragon likes word games. He's trying to figure out how many different words he can find in his name. We found fifteen, but there are more. You can mix up the letters but only use them once per word.

DINO
DRAGON

Dragon Boat

Dragon boats have the head of a dragon carved into the bow of the boat to give the paddlers strength while they race. But this is crazy. There are four heads! Can you see which is the fastest head?*

*The one with the most scales wins.

54

Dress-Up Dragon

Doris the dragon likes to dress up. What articles of clothing has she decided to wear? How are they different from the clothes she isn't wearing?

apron

baseball hat

sunglasses

pants

hoodie

down jacket

dress

leotard

shorts

socks

Singing Secret

Dragons don't like anybody to know it, but they love to sing. This little dragon has almost finished writing a song, but he is having trouble thinking of words that rhyme. Can you fill in the rest?

I can breathe f _ _ _

And one day I will learn to fly h _ _ _ _ _

As soon as I am brave enough to get off this w _ _ _ !

Why did dragons like to eat snowmen?

Because they melt in their mouth.

Dragon Breath

Talk about bad breath! Besides the usual fire-breathing, some dragons' breath is so cold it freezes enemies in their tracks and snaps them into pieces. Can you see what this was before the dragon breathed on it?

It's Jack the dragon's sixth birthday. It looks like a perfect sunny day, but can you find seven things wrong with this picture?

Magic Mirror

Finding a dragon in your living room has got to be pretty weird. Can you see anything else weird going on here? There are twelve changes in the mirror image on the right.

Dragons eat a wide variety of food. Their favorite drink is milk, which makes them very sleepy and relaxed. Other favorite foods include cakes, birds, oxen, deer, elephants, maidens, and princes.

According to ancient wisdom, if you have to win a case in court dragons can help. Place the fat of a dragon's heart in a gazelle skin and tie it to your arm with deer muscle. Now you are sure to win!

Wicked Ways

This wicked dragon has set a trap for anyone passing by his cave.
If you can figure out the clues, you may carry on your way.

1. The real bomb is in the column with a crown in it.

2. The real bomb does not have a heart in the same column.

3. The real bomb has a crown above it and beside it.

Receptionist: Doctor, there's an invisible dragon in the waiting room.

Doctor: Tell him I can't see him!

Dinosaur Versus Dragon

If a dragon fought a dinosaur, who do you think would win? We'll never know, but we can see in this before-and-after picture that some things have changed. Can you find nine?

Leafy Lair

Even though dragons weren't afraid of anybody, they sometimes had to hide. This dragon has covered himself with leaves. Can you count how many? To make it more fun, color in the leaves as you go.

DragonSlayers
Among other feats of bravery the ancient Greek heroes Apollo, Perseus, and Hercules are all said to have slain dragons.

Baby Beard

There is a real dragon that lives in Australia called the baby bearded dragon lizard. But this dragon is nothing like legendary ones. In fact, it is so gentle that it is one of the most popular reptiles to keep as a pet. Did you ever wonder what other reptiles would look like with a beard? Get your crayons and see!

Between the Eyes
If you ever have to feed a bearded dragon, the food should be about half the size of the distance between her eyes. So the bigger they get, the more food they get. Just like us!

It's possible somebody found fossil remains of a pterodactyl, which led them to believe they had found a dragon. Both had sharp beaks, huge wings, and the ability to fly. Can you tell which one of these pterodactyls is real? Unscramble the letters to find the one that spells the name properly.

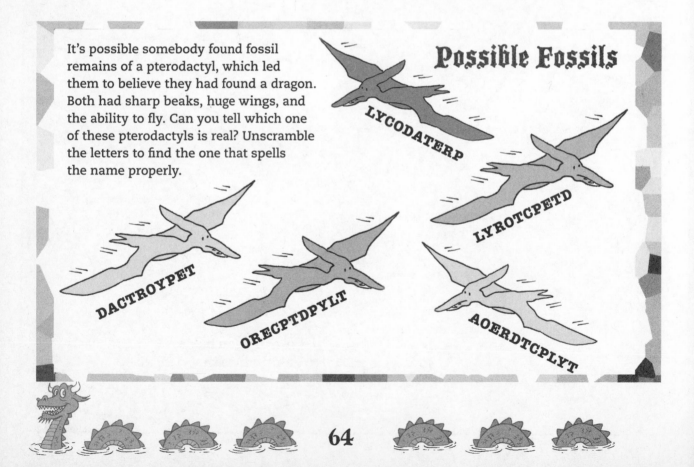

Possible Fossils

LYCODATERP

LYROTCPETD

DACTROYPET

ORECPTDPYLT

AOERDTCPLYT

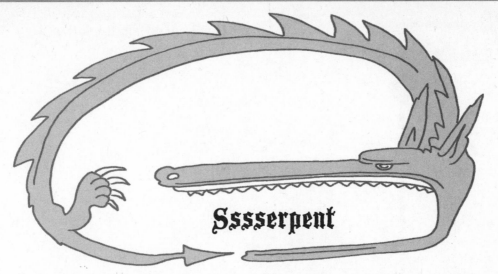

Sssserpent

Throughout history the words *serpent* and *dragon* are switched around, but they mean the same animal. This leads dragon experts to believe that people often confused snakes with dragons. Just as you would expect of a reptile, these serpents are very logical. Can you see what they will eat next?

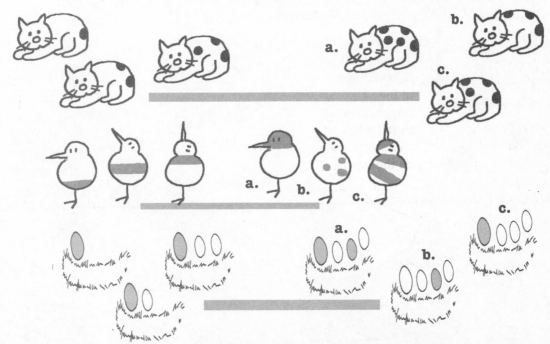

How do you know if a dragon has been in the fridge? Because there are footprints in the butter.

Crocodile Rock

In ancient times, facts were sometimes hard to come by. People wrote books and made drawings based on rumor and hearsay. One example was a book published in 1636 called *Collection of Quadrupeds*. An illustration shows what is called a dragon. Looking at it now we can tell it is actually a crocodile!

What animal do you think this is?

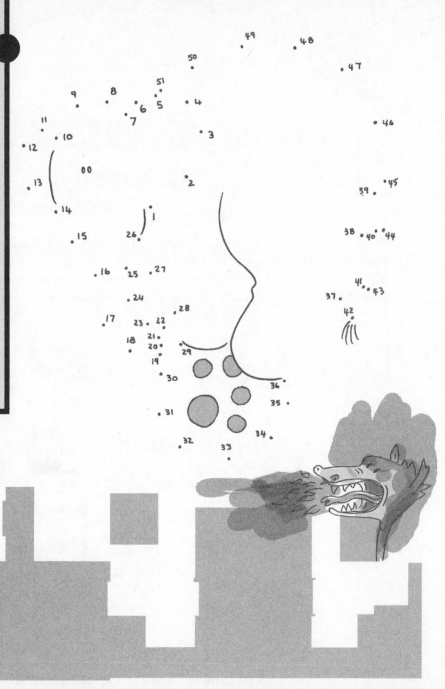

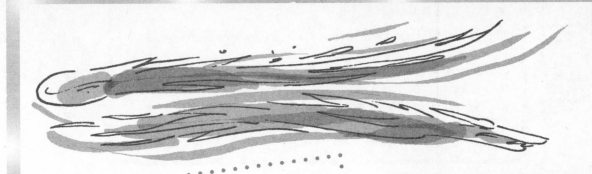

Elusive Fossils
The comet theory works well when we remember there have never been any dragon bones found even though dragon stories exist in most cultures.

_ O M _ _ _

_ O M _

_ O M _

_ _ _ O M

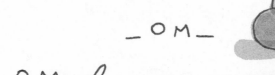

_ O M _

_ _ _ O M

Up in the Sky

Some people believe dragons were actually comets. It sounds crazy, but when you look closer it begins to makes sense. Dragons fly through the sky, they have a long body, a tail, and a head, and fire comes out of them. Just like a comet! Can you figure out what other words have something in common with comet?

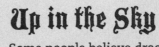

   67

Fly Dragon Fly

The dragonflies we know are quite small, but in prehistoric times they were as big as seagulls! Some people believe they could have been mistaken for dragons. Here's another trick for the eyes. Can you figure out what message this dragonfly left behind? Use the Shifting Letter Code as follows: A=B, B=C, C=D, D=E, E=F, F=G, G=H, H=I, I=J, J=K, K=L, L=M, M=N, N=O, O=P, P=Q, Q=R, R=S, S=T, T=U, U=V, V=W, W=X, X=Y, Y=Z, Z=A

CQZFNM OZQSX

SNMHFGS!

FIRE AWAY

In the Middle Ages people believed that animals were not harmed by fire and could even be reborn in it.

Fearsome Flower

The snapdragon, seen from a distance, appears to have a big red mouth with a bright yellow tongue. If you're a bit sleepy, it could even appear to have flames coming out. Here are some flowers that look pretty tame. Can you make them look like fearsome monsters?

Here are a few tools to help you!

angry eyebrows crazy eyes pointy teeth grrrr lines

All at Sea

This dragon is rarely seen because of its great camouflage, but it really exists off the coast of Australia. Male sea dragons carry the eggs until they hatch. Can you make out what he's saying?

Just Believe

To some people, it's still a mystery whether dragons really exist. Can you solve this mystery? Here's a clue: Each letter has been shifted either up or down. The letter B could be written as either A or C.

Which Way?

If dragons existed they had to be pretty smart. In the East they were worshipped for their wisdom. In the West, where they were hunted, they managed to stick around for hundreds of years. How well can you do in this game? Can you predict which object will come next?

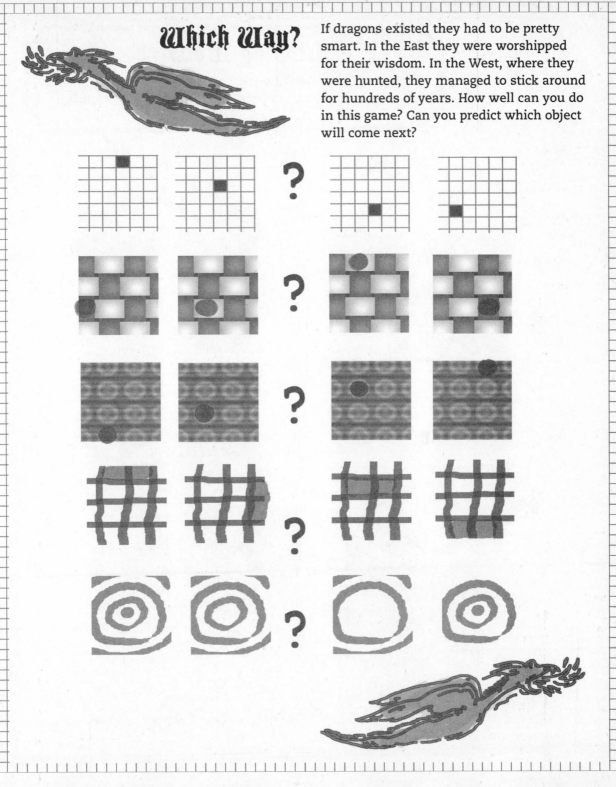

Missing Monster

These dragons are all missing a piece. Can you put them back together? Just draw a line to where the right piece should go.

Flag Waving

The Welsh flag is believed to be the oldest national flag in the world. It proudly carries the image of a dragon.

No Bones about It!

Although no dragon remains have ever been found, it is believed the bones would have been hollow or of a very light material. This would allow them to fly. Dragons have some other unique features.

Can you figure out which one of these skulls belonged to a dragon? He sure has a lot on his mind! It must have one each of the following:

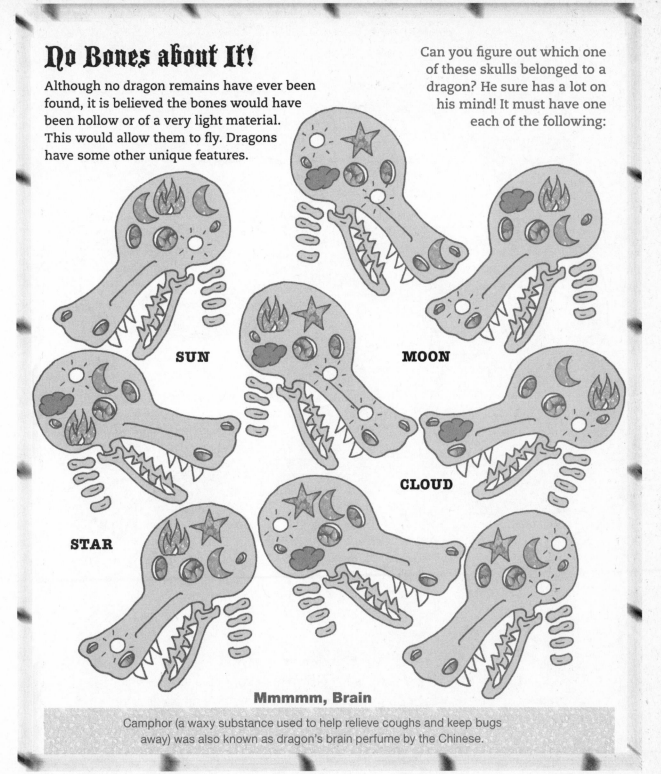

SUN

MOON

CLOUD

STAR

Mmmmm, Brain

Camphor (a waxy substance used to help relieve coughs and keep bugs away) was also known as dragon's brain perfume by the Chinese.

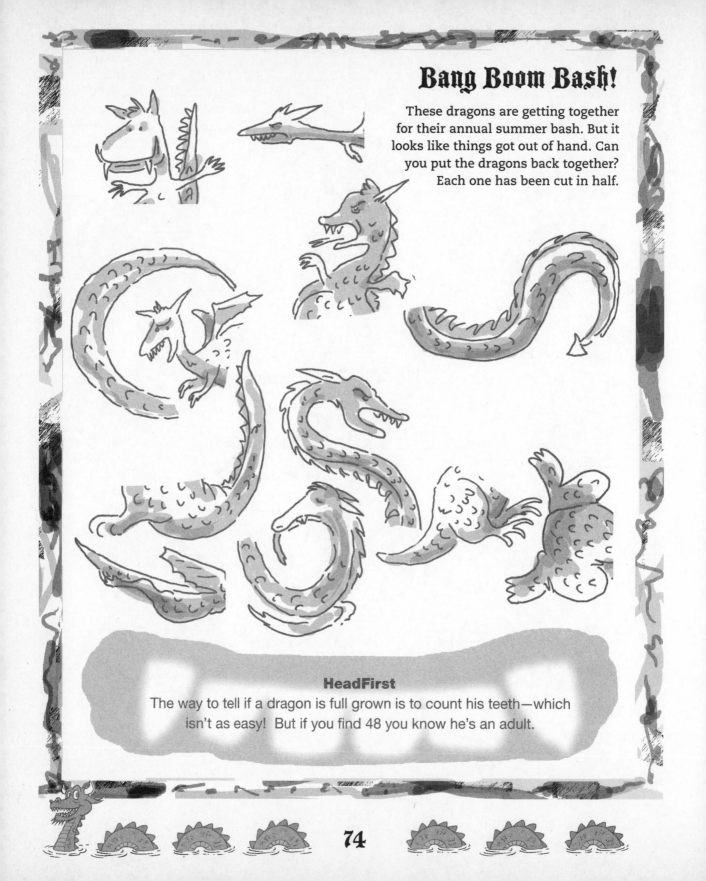

Bang Boom Bash!

These dragons are getting together for their annual summer bash. But it looks like things got out of hand. Can you put the dragons back together? Each one has been cut in half.

HeadFirst
The way to tell if a dragon is full grown is to count his teeth—which isn't as easy! But if you find 48 you know he's an adult.

It's a Bird, It's a Dragon

Dragons hate it when people confuse them with birds, so they have some other names that mean "dragon." Can you figure out what they are? There is one letter repeated in each word. Cross it out to reveal these cool dragon names.

Seeerepeeeneet

Feieeree bereeaeteheeer

Keoemeoedeoe

Teyepeheoen

What do you get when you take a dragon to school?

An empty school!

Where There's Smoke

The most famous and fearsome dragons are the fire-breathing ones. You have to be very brave to fight one of these monsters. Could you face a fire-breathing dragon with just a sword and shield?

Dragon Decorations
Dragons were sometimes used to decorate shields to show the warrior's strength. Can you find the two shields that are exactly alike?

Steam Heat

Dragons that can't breathe fire do the next best thing—steam heat! If you've gotten your hand near a steaming kettle, you know it's hot! This dragon has other differences. Follow the directions to see what he wants to be.

Replace the A
with a Y.

Make a space
after the Y.

Replace the GO
with CLEA.

Add ER
after the N.

Dragon Song

Have you ever had a song written about you? Tons of dragons have. They are called ballads. One of the most famous is about Tiamat, the Great Goddess dragon. She created the skies with a breath and the earth with her body. You can make your own song too. We've collected some words for you. Just add one story, stir, and have fun!

scale	gold
whale	old
tale	told
tail	wing
talon	ring
armor	sing
fire	sky
breathe	fly
teeth	

Smart Serpent!

Now this is cool! Dragons live for hundreds of years and are very intelligent. This smart dragon loves math. He's using subtraction clues to figure out how to get into the magic kingdom next door to his cave.

A = 1	F = 6	L = 12	S = 19
B = 2	G = 7	M = 13	T = 20
C = 3	H = 8	N = 14	U = 21
D = 4	I = 9	O = 15	V = 22
E = 5	J = 10	P = 16	W = 23
	K = 11	Q = 17	X = 24
		R = 18	Y = 25
			Z = 26

$10 + 9 =$ ___ $5 - 4 =$ ___ $5 \times 5 =$ ___

$2 \times 8 =$ ___ $15 - 3 =$ ___ $20 - 15 =$ ___

$38 - 37 =$ ___ $3 \times 6 + 1 =$ ___

$7 - 3 + 1 =$ ___

Look out for That Tail!

In Africa there is a legend about dragons and elephants. It is said that elephants give birth in water to avoid being attacked by the tail of the dragon.

Dragon Magic

Along with doing magic tricks (which is pretty impressive), some dragons can speak our language. What do you suppose they would say?

SPEAKING DRAGONESE

See if you can figure out what this dragon is saying. He seems to be having trouble with the first letter of every word.

ragons ance owntown

ervous urses otice oise

ig ears uild arns

Frosty the Dragon

What do you call a frozen dragon?

A dragsicle.

Ahead of Its Time

One of the most interesting types of dragon had many heads. Can you do a head count here? This dragon seems to have some extra. How many don't belong?

Knock Knock!

Who's there?

Howl.

Howl who?

Howl we escape from this dragon cave?

Just Big

Sometimes just being big impresses people. In the Bible, there is a dragon so enormous that with one sweep of his tail he could remove a third of the stars in the heavens.

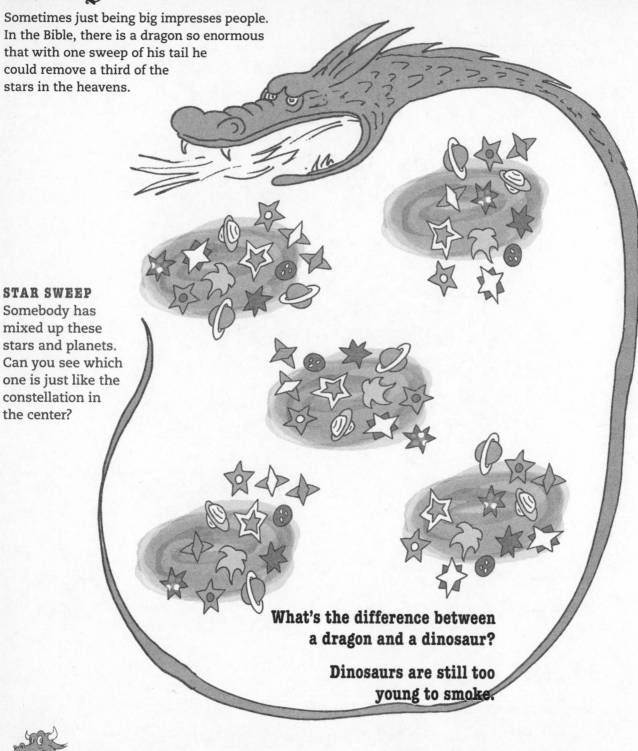

STAR SWEEP
Somebody has mixed up these stars and planets. Can you see which one is just like the constellation in the center?

What's the difference between a dragon and a dinosaur?

Dinosaurs are still too young to smoke.

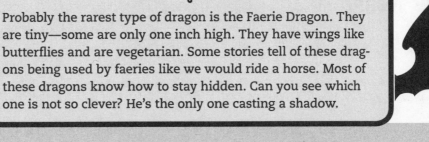

Just Small

Probably the rarest type of dragon is the Faerie Dragon. They are tiny—some are only one inch high. They have wings like butterflies and are vegetarian. Some stories tell of these dragons being used by faeries like we would ride a horse. Most of these dragons know how to stay hidden. Can you see which one is not so clever? He's the only one casting a shadow.

What do you get when you cross a dragon with a dog?

A very nervous postman.

Boom Boom Dragoon

There used to be a firearm called a musket (a type of rifle) that shot flames as it fired. This was nicknamed the Dragon. There are five each of different weapons here—except for one. Can you figure out which one only shows up four times?

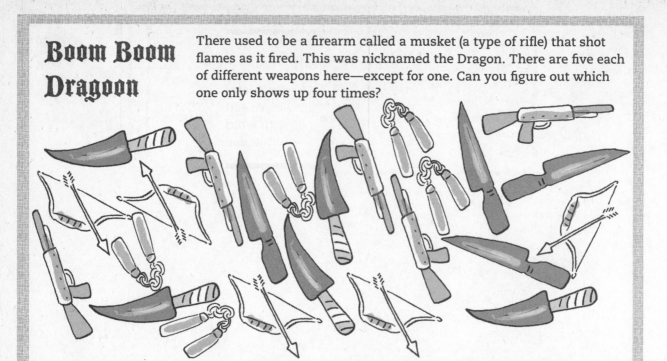

Bits and Pieces

Some dragons look like they are made up of different things put together.
You can do the same with words. What common word goes with the three samples given?

_ _ _ _ hunter

_ _ _ _ ache

fore_ _ _ _

base_ _ _ _

_ _ _ _ oon

_ _ _ _ park

_ _ _ _ onfly

_ _ _ _ net

_ _ _ _ on

_ _ _ port

_ _ _ plane

_ _ _ mattress

_ _ _ _ mobile

_ _ _ _ matic

_ _ _ _ graph

Wardrobe Mixup

This is one popular dragon. He needs lots of clothes to wear, but somehow his outfits have gotten mixed up. Can you see which hat goes with which T-shirt? Be careful. There are some extras that don't match.

Fighting Knight

Sometimes knights would be gone for weeks when they went out to fight dragons. Can you see what this knight is bringing with him?

 + or

 + case

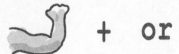 + chet

When the knights would engage in combat with a dragon they would have to see the whites of their eyes—except dragons are usually shown as having large yellow or red eyes with pupils that were narrow slits.

 + 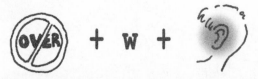 es

c +    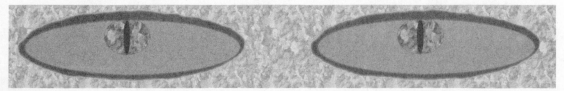 + w +

   **86**

Dragon Day Care

These dragon parents have come to pick up their babies. But there are way more babies than parents, and it's hard to tell who belongs to who. Can you tell from the markings which parent belongs to which baby?

Oroboros

Oroboros means "tail-eater." Some dragons are shown this way in old paintings. They are the symbol of eternity.

Cave Sweet Cave

This explorer is leaving a trail. Read the clues in the center to fill in the blanks. The last letter of one word is the first letter of the next. Now you can see what kind of cave this is.

1. Not a window but a . . . _____

2. A girl's name that rhymes with soda
_____

3. Getting older
_____

4. A type of dance
_____

5. Where you cook
_____

6. More than want
_____

7. Type of deer
_____

8. Equal
_____

9. Not old
_____

5. __

6. __

4. __

7. __

8 __

3. __

1 _____
2 _____
3 _____
4 _____
5 _____
6 _____
7 _____
8 _____
9

9. __

2. __

1. __

In the West most dragons lived in caves. In the East they lived in or near the water.

Lucky House

In China, having a dragon in your home is good luck. A dragon represents abundance and good fortune. Chinese people say they are "Lung Tik Chuan Ren," which means descendents of the dragon. How many dragons can you see decorating this lucky home?

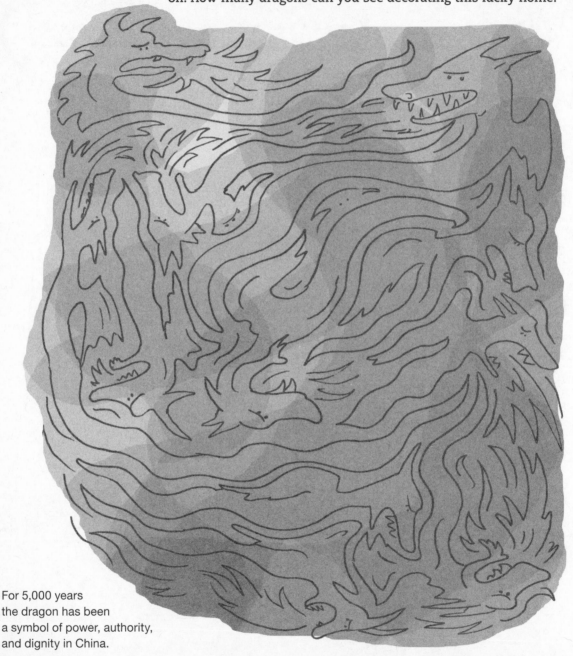

For 5,000 years the dragon has been a symbol of power, authority, and dignity in China.

Dragon Worship

In the East most dragons lived in the water. Today you will still find shrines and altars scattered along lake shores and riversides. That way people could be close to the dragons when they asked for favors. Each dot represents a shrine. Can you tell what the people were visiting?

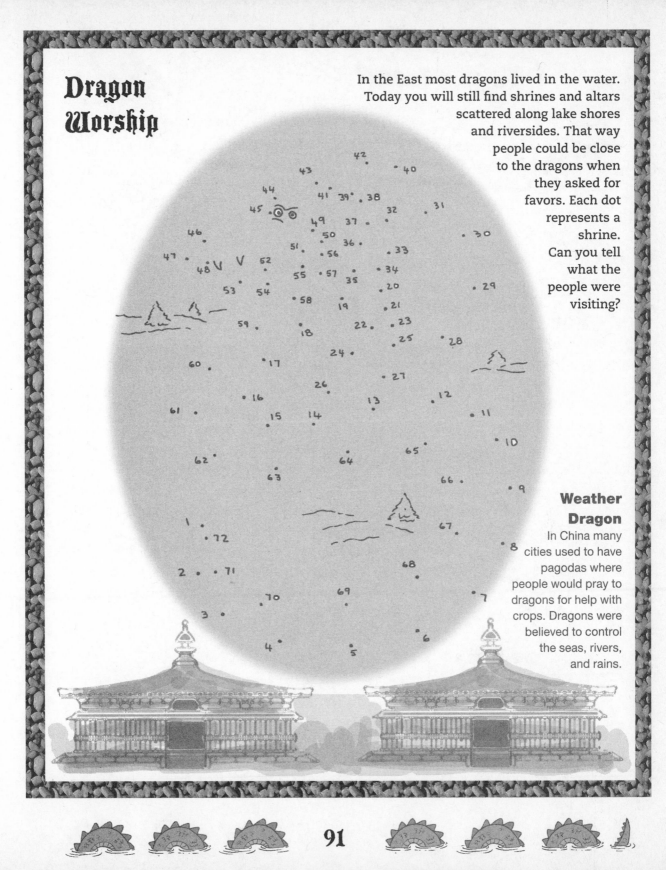

Weather Dragon

In China many cities used to have pagodas where people would pray to dragons for help with crops. Dragons were believed to control the seas, rivers, and rains.

Boulder Dinner

How would you like stones for dinner? Dragons have such strong acid in their stomachs that they can digest boulders! Here's some other words with "ou" in them. Do you think dragons could eat these?

_ ou _ _ _ _ _ _

_ ou _ _

_ ou _ _ _ _ _

_ ou _ _
_ ou _ _ _ _ _

How do you make a dragon float?

Two scoops of ice cream, soda water, a dragon, and a cherry on top!

_ _ ou _

_ ou _ _

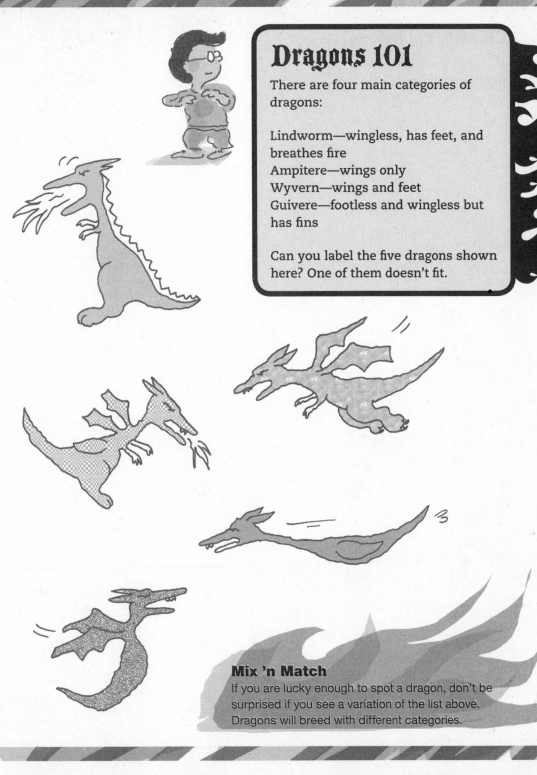

Dragons 101

There are four main categories of dragons:

Lindworm—wingless, has feet, and breathes fire
Ampitere—wings only
Wyvern—wings and feet
Guivere—footless and wingless but has fins

Can you label the five dragons shown here? One of them doesn't fit.

Mix 'n Match
If you are lucky enough to spot a dragon, don't be surprised if you see a variation of the list above. Dragons will breed with different categories.

Decorating Dragon

This dragon loves to decorate. He's just bought a lamp and covered it with leaves. How many can you count?

Cave Confusion

There are too many caves! Can you help this cold dragon find his way back to the cave with the fire?

Monster Mash

Dragons could eat just about anything, from crispy knights to boulder soup. Can you figure out what this dragon has ordered? Fill in all the letters that are not H, M, A, I, E, S, D, and R, and read what's left.

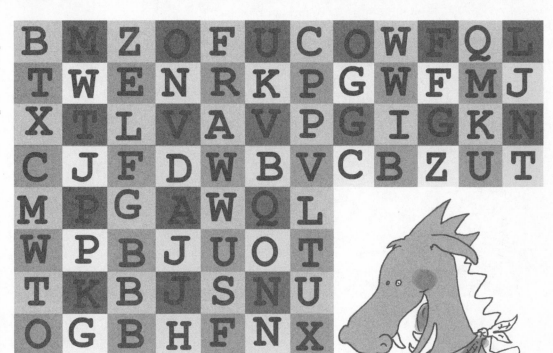

Mom AND Dad
In 2006 a Komodo called Flora gave birth to five babies even though she had never had contact with a male Komodo. This strange occurrence is called parthenogenesis.

95

Dinner Daydream

This dragon is so hungry he's dreaming of dinner. But this dream doesn't make sense. Can you put the pieces back together and see what kind of dinner dragons like best?

Imagine you're trapped in a dragon's cave and he's blocking your way out. What do you do?

Stop imagining!

Dragon Tail

Here's a fun game called Dragon's Tail. Draw a shape like this with some chalk—make sure each box is big enough to fit your feet into. Just like in hopscotch, a player hops from space to space on one foot, starting on the outside space. When you reach the middle you can rest on both feet, then turn around and hop back on one foot to the start. If you make it both ways without stepping on a line or touching both feet to the ground, write your name in one space of your choosing. That space is then called your scale (just like on a dragon's tail). On your next turn you can rest both feet on that scale. The player with the most scales at the end of the game is the winner.

To make it more of a challenge, other players have to jump over your scale. Only you can jump on it.

This dragon is scarier than most. Can you see why?

Here's a hint: turn the book upside down and have another look.

Quarter Question

Dragons are extremely wise, but this little guy is having trouble with his glasses. Can you help him figure out which quarter of each circle is not like the rest?

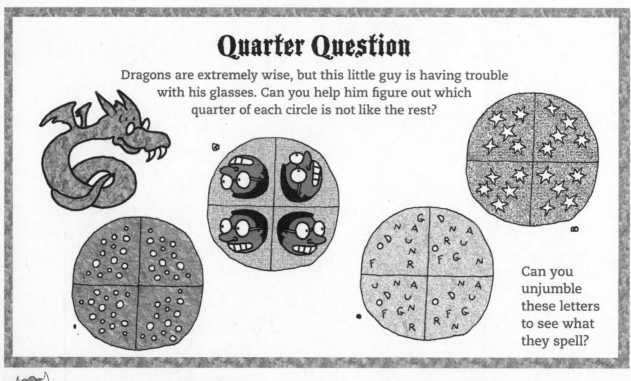

Can you unjumble these letters to see what they spell?

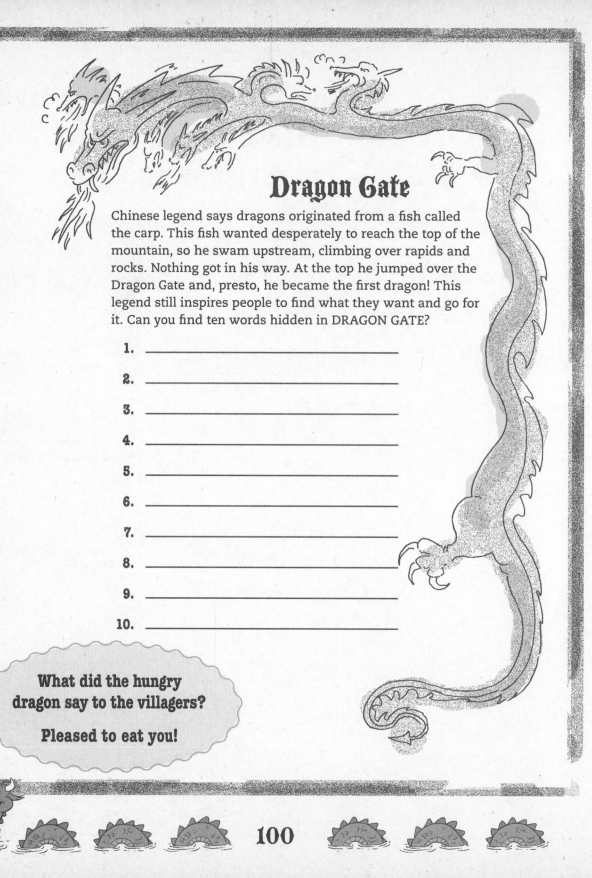

Dragon Gate

Chinese legend says dragons originated from a fish called the carp. This fish wanted desperately to reach the top of the mountain, so he swam upstream, climbing over rapids and rocks. Nothing got in his way. At the top he jumped over the Dragon Gate and, presto, he became the first dragon! This legend still inspires people to find what they want and go for it. Can you find ten words hidden in DRAGON GATE?

1. _____

2. _____

3. _____

4. _____

5. _____

6. _____

7. _____

8. _____

9. _____

10. _____

What did the hungry dragon say to the villagers?

Pleased to eat you!

100

Naughty Dragons

It looks like this mischievous drag-on has got into the professor's room and messed up the words.

Can you match these big words with their correct meanings?

voracious	bizarre
omnivorous	wicked
fantastical	hungry
serpentine	eats many different kinds of foods
malevolent	twisting

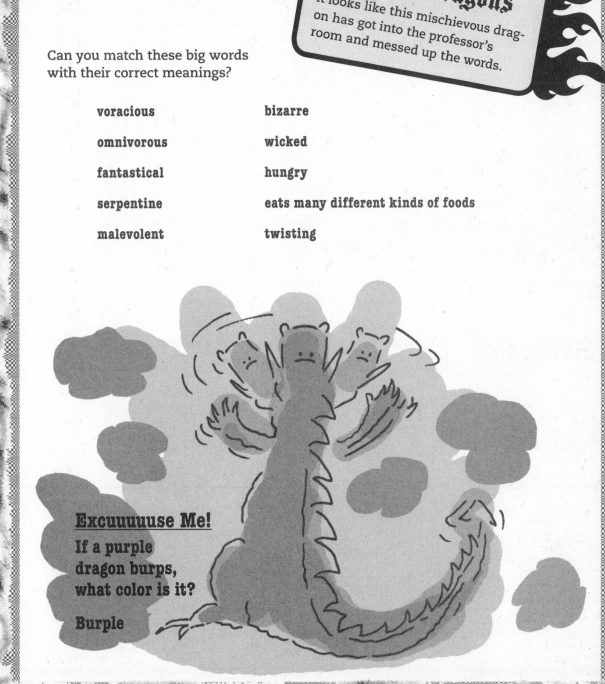

Excuuuuuse Me!

If a purple dragon burps, what color is it?

Burple

   101

Giant Words

For a dragon it's hard finding playmates the same size. Luckily there were giants roaming around. They played on HUGE playgrounds with HUGE footballs. Here are some words that mean huge. Someone has replaced the Es and As with other vowels. Can you figure them out?

onormous _____

gigontic _____

missivu _____

gorgintuon _____

colossil _____

immonsu _____

What do you call a person who is brave enough to stick his right hand into a dragon's mouth?
Lefty

Ra Ra Ra!

Dragons needed encouragement just like anybody else. Too bad there weren't cheerleaders in medieval times.

These words all have the letters "RA" in them. Can you figure out what they are?

_ ra _ _

_ ra _ _ _ _

_ ra _ _

_ ra _

_ _ ra _ _

_ ra _ _

Dragon Discussion

It's possible that dragons had their own alphabet. Here's a message scratched on the cave wall. Can you make out what it says? Look at the code below to help figure it out.

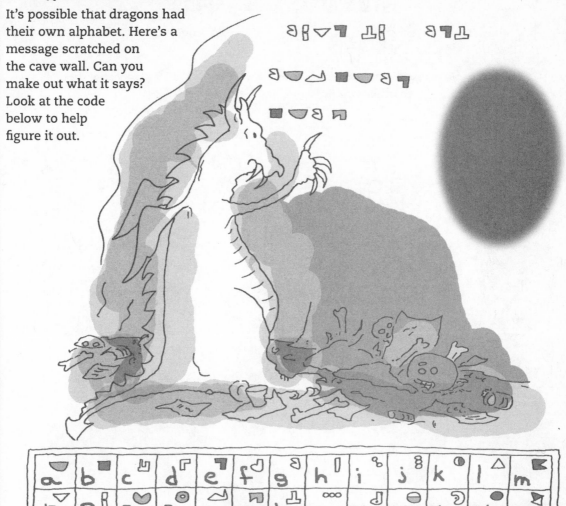

You can make your own alphabet code, too. Here are a few examples to get you started.

Gruesome Dragsome

What an organized dragon! He wants to put everything in the proper order. Can you tell what comes next?

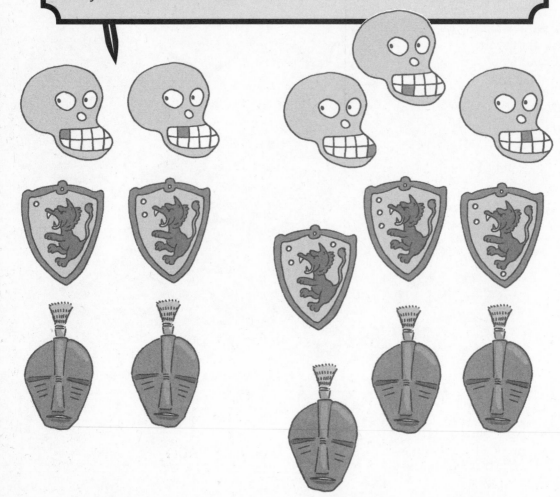

How can you tell if a dragon is under your bed?

Your nose is touching the ceiling!

Precious Plunder

In medieval times, there was an ongoing battle between the king and the local dragons. These dragons have just returned from attacking the king's palace. They stole precious jewels and weapons. There are five dragons, so there should be five of everything—but there are only four of some things. Can you see which ones?

DDDDRAGONS
Here's a fun tongue twister you can do with your friends. Try taking turns saying this three times fast: "Did you know dirty dragons dawdle as they doodle?"

Dragon Tricks

Dragons have a whole bag of tricks and tools they use to scare people and win battles. Can you unscramble these words to see what they are?

Now put the capital letters in order to find out what scares dragons the most!

awlsc

reIf

aror

sEplsl

gamCi

kMoes

solatn

In Chinese mythology there are four dragon kings, one for each of the four directions: North, South, East, and West.

Fierce Fake

Dragons were known to have a foul temper. None of these dragons is too friendly, but one in particular really doesn't fit. Can you find the nasty dragon with the following: a beard, three teeth in its top jaw and two on the bottom, three claws, and a hat with three dots.

Fire and Water

In the West, if you get a dragon angry he will probably burn down your village. In the East, an angry dragon would cause flooding or torrential downpours.

   107

Hats Off

This dragon needs a new hat. Find the one with the following characteristics:

three stripes, one circle, no triangle, and one square.

Dragon for a Day

Imagine you were a dragon for a day. What would you do? Write down five things, and remember you can breathe fire and fly!

CHAPTER 10
Dot-to-Dot Dragons

Big Baby

When you're a baby animal, you have to know how to hide and stay out of danger. Dragons might be almost impossible to kill once they're fully grown, but baby dragons are a different story. Can you see these baby dragons? They have good camouflage.

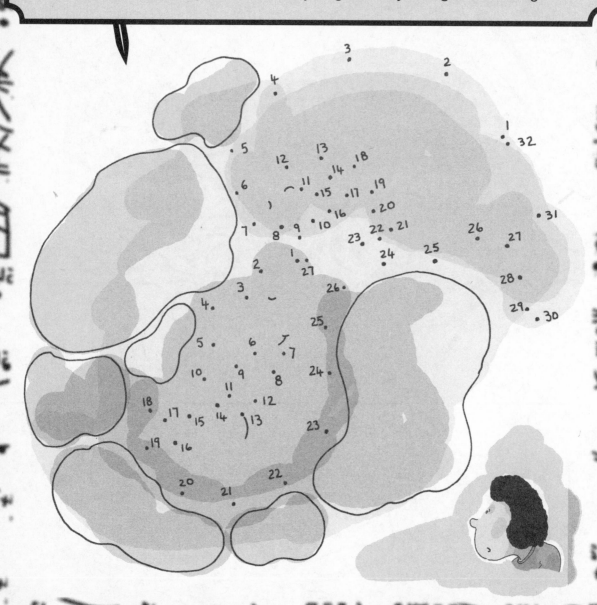

Egg-citing

Dragon babies hatch from eggs just like dinosaurs and birds. This one looks pretty helpless—just like a human baby. Dragons start out walking on all fours until they begin to get their balance.

I have a little house in which I live all alone. My house has no doors or windows, and if I want to go out I must break through the wall. What am I?

An egg!

Bigfoot!

How big do you think a dragon's foot would be? As big as an elephant's foot? Even bigger? Connect the dots to find the one footprint that doesn't belong to a dragon. (Hint: Maybe it belongs to Bigfoot!)

Sharpen Up!

Have you ever wondered what it would be like to have a dragon teaching your class? It might be kind of cool to have a teacher who could breathe fire! But you wouldn't want to make her angry! Connect the dots to see what might happen if you ran out of chalk!

Dragon Websites

There's lots of information about dragons on the Internet!
Go online to learn more about these amazing creatures.

webtech.kennesaw.edu/jcheek3/dragons.htm
Want to find some artifacts or learn how to draw dragons? This site has it all.

www.dmbh.org/portal/dragon_information/information_sites.html
This site is called Dragons Must Be Here. It's full of information and fun. This site is a directory to other dragon sites as well as a great resource.

www.lair2000.net
Be careful when you visit this Dragon's Lair. There's music, so make sure your computer's volume control isn't set too loud. It's a bit heavy on the graphics, but there are still lots of great things to learn.

www.bestiarium.net/select.html
This is a dragon site from Germany, but there are lots of pages in English—and even the German pages have great pictures to look at.

www.dragonmuse.com/lore1-1.html
You can tell the person who put this website up really loves dragons.

uktv.co.uk/documentary/stepbystep/aid/588092
This site is about Komodo dragons only, but there are some fascinating facts.

www.draconian.com/special-life1/life.htm
Draconian is a bit more scientific than some of the other sites. Ever wondered how long it takes a dragon to grow up to be an adult?

www.dragonorama.com
This is a great all-purpose dragon site covering everything you could ever want to know.

APPENDIX B
Puzzle Solutions

CHAPTER 1: DRAGONOLOGY: A HISTORY OF DRAGONS

St. George the Gentleman • page 3

Tail in Mouth • page 5

There are thirty-four circles. Don't forget the earth and Jormungand!

Elephants for Dinner • page 6

Ring of the Nibelung • page 4

PUZZLE SOLUTIONS

Beowulf Versus the Dragon • page 7

Go away, I am making
magic soup!

Smaug • page 8
On his left chest

The World Tree • page 9

A R<u>oo</u>F is on top of the house.

If you cut yourself you see BL<u>oo</u>D.

We need to eat F<u>oo</u>D to survive.

When you look in the night sky you
can see the M<u>oo</u>N.

If a dragon is attacking, SH<u>oo</u>T your arrow at him!

To sweep his cave a dragon needs a good BR<u>oo</u>M.

The GR<u>oo</u>M kissed the bride.

When you eat soup a SP<u>oo</u>N is helpful.

A big motorbike goes VR<u>oo</u>M!

Dragons are featured in some CART<u>oo</u>NS.

Terrified Townsfolk • page 10

Too Many Heads • page 11

116

PUZZLE SOLUTIONS

Careful Counting • page 12

2000 shows up eight times on this dragon

Mississippi Mane • page 13

Horrific Heralic • page 13

This dragon is 310 years old

Stormy Sayings • page 14

BEWARE THE COMING STORM

CHAPTER 2: EVERYBODY'S GOT A DRAGON

Ancient Courage • page 16

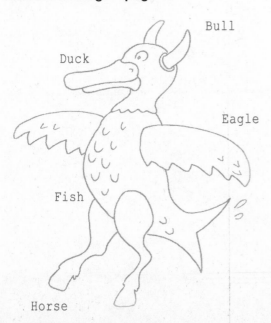

Bull

Duck

Eagle

Fish

Horse

Norse Numbers • page 17

Twelve dragons

PUZZLE SOLUTIONS

Greek Guard Dog • page 18

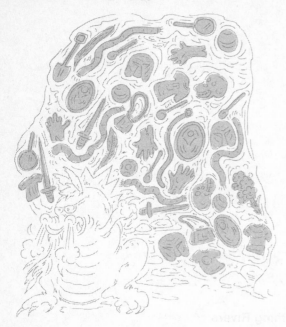

Horse and All • page 19

fall	ball
king	ring
large	barge
blue	glue

Cherokee Crystal • page 19

The first letter of each
word has been put at the end
of each word. Just put it
back in the front and the
message is clear.

DO NOT ANGER ME OR YOUR VILLAGE WILL BE
DESTROYED!

All for One • page 20

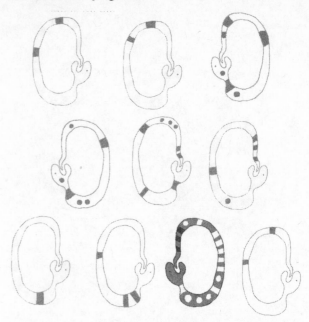

All the words are made up of letters contained in
the word *dragon*.

Rockin' Russia • page 21

PUZZLE SOLUTIONS

Mexican Monster • page 22

18 coins   This coin appears most often.

10 coins

12 coins

10 coins

1 coin   This coin appears only once.

There are five different types of coins.

There are nineteen heads.

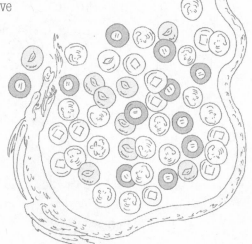

Come on, Komodo! • page 23

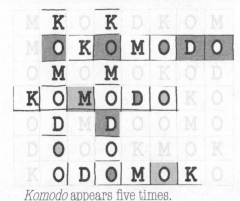

Komodo appears five times.

Dragon Digits • page 24

There are five Japanese dragons.

Writing Rivers • page 26

S	I	L	F	L	M	F	S
A	F	D	E	L	L	S	T
L	H	E	L	L	M	O	F
U	N	L	T	F	F	A	I
L	L	N	S	F	F	S	S

I MADE THE MOUNTAIN

Abraxas to Zu • page 26

Brinsop was a dangerous dragon in England. According to legend, he was killed by St. George.

E	T	L	L	M	P	S	E	A	A	U
B	F	G	C	E	E	D	G	H	R	J
K	Q	T	U	T	V	A	M	W	W	Y
A	C	W	X	X	I	D	E	H	H	U
W	N	F	E	E	H	A	A	M	Q	T
V	V	W	B	Z	Z	M	H	H	S	E
T	T	O	K	K	T	E	F	B	A	A
C	D	G	H	W	W	J	P	K	L	M

119

PUZZLE SOLUTIONS

Princess Pal • page 28

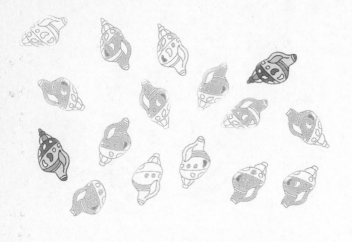

Which Witch? • page 30

Heave and
weave and
spoil and toil!
Trouble and bubble
will follow YOU!
If you don't heed
my words, Druid the
dragon will fly over
and fire YOU!

Watch Out, Wizard! • page 29

The ten changes: sun, eyes on the skull, mouse hole, mouse, book stand, key, moon on the hat, flame under the flask, stripes on the lizard, open eye on the dragon

Meet the Mermaid • page 31

ruby
diam**O**nds
garnet
emera**L**d
sapphire
Amethyst
Pearl

OPAL

PUZZLE SOLUTIONS

Day and Knight • page 32

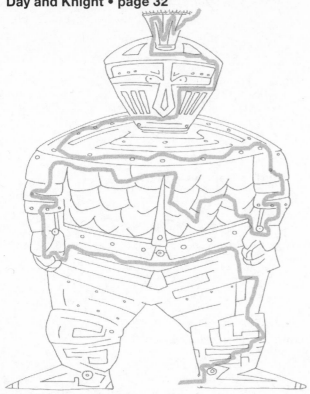

Gggggriffins • page 34

ROOFTOPS

Bird's-Eye View • page 34

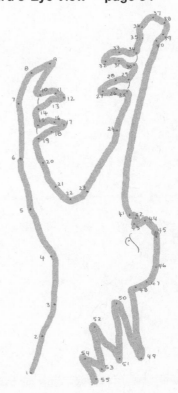

Fake Fairies • page 33

PUZZLE SOLUTIONS

King's Ransom • page 35

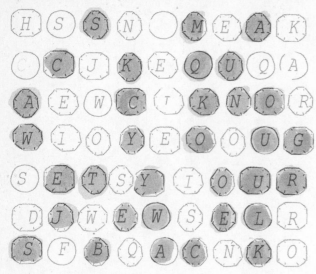

Smack, quack, now you get your jewels back!

Flying Fire • page 36

Adapt a Dragon • page 37

steam, team
smile, mile
steak, teak
table, able
clock, lock

Hand to Head • page 37

Each hat can be worn with six possible pairs of gloves, and there are five hats. The answer is 6 x 5, which equals 30 combinations.

Unicorn or Not • page 38

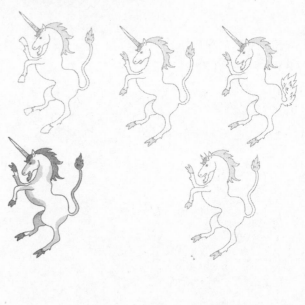

PUZZLE SOLUTIONS

CHAPTER 4: FROM DRAGONET TO WYRM

Straight from the Egg • page 40

Alan, Beckham, Casey, Doris, Elaine, Fred, Gerry, Hannah, Isadora, Jessica, Kim, Leon, Matthew, Norman, Orville, Petra, Queenie, River, Sonny, Travis, Uma, Victoria, Wendy, Xanadu, Yasmin, Zephyr

The character's name is Draco Malfoy.

Goo Goo • page 41

First Steps • page 42

It's time for baby to go to bed.

Careful, Baby! • page 42

There are eleven "fires."

PUZZLE SOLUTIONS

Alphadragon • page 43

OWL
PARACHUTE
IGLOO
GOOSE
HOUSE
UMBRELLA
WINDOW
X MARKS THE SPOT
QUEEN
LADDER
ZEBRA
BALL
SNAKE
FROG
YAK
DOG
VASE
KING
JUMP ROPE
CAT TURTLE
RABBIT
EGG
NEST
MOUSE
ANT

Teenage Trouble • page 44

I WILL SAVE YOUR VILLAGE IF YOU BRING ME CHOCOLATE.

Young Love • page 45

angry

sleepy

sad

confused

surprised

Dragon Wings • page 46

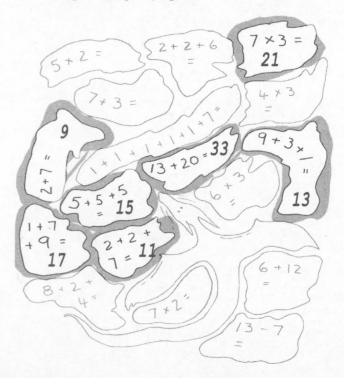

$5 + 2 =$

$2 + 2 + 6 =$

$7 \times 3 = \mathbf{21}$

$7 + 3 =$

$4 \times 3 =$

9

$2 + 7 =$

$1 + 1 + 1 + 1 + 1 + 1 + 7 =$

$13 + 20 = \mathbf{33}$

$9 + 3 \times 1 =$

$5 + 5 + 5 = \mathbf{15}$

$6 \times 3 =$

13

$1 + 7 + 9 = \mathbf{17}$

$2 + 2 + 7 = \mathbf{11}$

$8 + 2 + 4 =$

$6 + 12 =$

$7 \times 2 =$

$13 - 7 =$

PUZZLE SOLUTIONS

Drawing Dragons • page 47

The one vulnerable spot on a dragon is the stomach.

It's in the Stars • page 48

ACROSS
1: Lucky
2: Artist
3: Help
4: On
5: Great

DOWN
A: Active
B: Top
C: Caring

Go Dragon, Go! • page 49

Not badness but GOODNESS

GOLDILOCKS and the three bears

A boy's name: GORDON

This bird honks: GOOSE

The great GOLD rush

Dark blue is known as INDIGO

If you are going to the ball you wear a GOWN

The Disney dog with big ears: GOOFY

Crazy Crowns • page 50

PUZZLE SOLUTIONS

CHAPTER 5: FIVE-HEADED, FIRE-BREATHING DRAGON SEEKS SAME

Dragon Detective • page 52

Dragon Spell • page 54

Here are some of the words
you can find in "DINO DRAGON."

noon	dog	raid
grin	drain	rid
groan	ran	rag
drag	gain	grand
dig	rain	grid

Dragon Boat • page 54

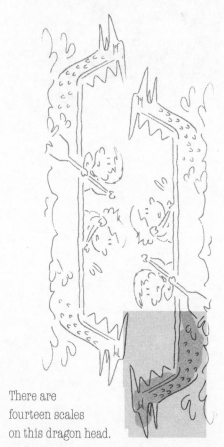

There are
fourteen scales
on this dragon head.

Your Indoor Voice • page 53

L O O U P L E O S E
Y U O T P E P L Y K
U P N E E S E N O Y
U O **P L E A S E** Y B
B P P L E S T Y T Y
N L T T G G S U S H
O E H T J I O T S Y
S A O E A P R G R H
H O G F G I R E F T
T H A N K   Y O U S G
Y O Y T H A A S E R
U U U K Y S A S E F

PUZZLE SOLUTIONS

Dress-Up Dragon • page 55

All the words have the letter D in them.

Singing Secret • page 56

I can breathe fire
And one day I will
learn to fly higher
As soon as I am brave
enough to get off
this wire!

Dragon Breath • page 57

Happy Birthday, Dragon! • page 57

1. "Birthday" is spelled wrong.
2. There are seven candles.
3. There are icicles in the summer.
4. His name is Jack, not Joey.
5. It's noon but the sun is setting.
6. The cat is barking.

Magic Mirror • page 58

1. The tree isn't the same.
2. There is no sun.
3. The third banner is different.
4. The last circle on the cornice above the third banner is filled in.
5. There is no crown on the person peeking around the corner.
6. The doorknockers are upside down.
7. The stairs are missing a top step.
8. The pedestal for the candle is missing a middle circle.
9. The picture of the lion doesn't have teeth.
10. The corner of the carpet is missing a circle.
11. The lady in front of the dragon has a different apron.
12. The boy in front of the dragon has a different hat.

Wicked Ways • page 60

127

PUZZLE SOLUTIONS

Dinosaur Versus Dragon • page 61

1. The dragon's snout doesn't have scales.
2. The dragon doesn't have a tongue.
3. Part of the dragon's wing is missing.
4. The dragon's tail isn't as long.
5. The dinosaur's eye is different.
6. The dinosaur is missing a tooth.
7. The dinosaur's tongue is a different color.
8. The dinosaur's tail is missing a white stripe.
9. The dinosaur is missing a toenail.

Leafy Lair • page 61

There are 20 leaves on the dragon

CHAPTER 6: DRAGON BONES

Possible Fossils • page 64

aoerdtcplyt = pterodactyl

Sssserpent • page 65

PUZZLE SOLUTIONS

Crocodile Rock • page 66

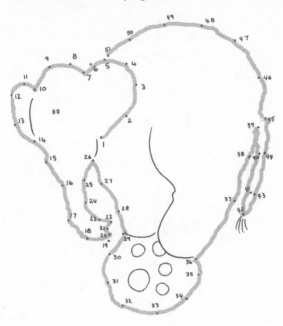

Up in the Sky • page 67

ROMAN

DOME

BOMB

BROOM

HOME

VROOM

Fly Dragon Fly • page 68

DRAGON PARTY TONIGHT!

All at Sea • page 70

Hold the page upside down in front of a mirror to discover what he's saying.

I AM EXPECTING 250 BABIES IN A COUPLE OF WEEKS?

Just Believe • page 70

WE EXIST IF YOU BELIEVE IN US!

Which Way? • page 71

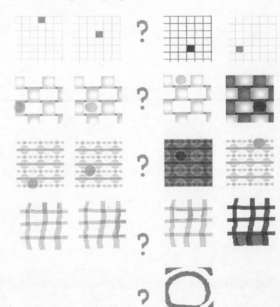

PUZZLE SOLUTIONS

Missing Monster • page 72

No Bones about It! • page 73

Bang Boom Bash! • page 74

PUZZLE SOLUTIONS

It's a Bird, It's a Dragon • page 76

Serpent
Fire Breather
Komodo
Typhon

Where There's Smoke • page 77

Steam Heat • page 78

DRY CLEANER

Smart Serpent! • page 79

19, 1, 25, 16, 12 , 5, 1, 19, 5
When you change the letters to numbers, you come
up with the answer: say please!

Dragon Magic • page 80

Dragons Dance Downtown
Nervous Nurses Notice Noise
Big Bears Build Barns

Ahead of Its Time • page 81

Just Big • page 82

PUZZLE SOLUTIONS

Just Small • page 83

Boom Boom Dragoon • page 84

Bits and Pieces • page 84

Airport

Airplane

Air mattress

Automobile

Automatic

Autograph

Headhunter

Headache

Forehead

Baseball

Balloon

Ballpark

Dragonfly

Dragnet

Dragon

Wardrobe Mixup • page 85

Fighting Knight • page 86

+ or *armor*

+ case *suitcase*

+ chet *hatchet*

+ es *sandwiches*

c + OVER + w + *clean underwear*

PUZZLE SOLUTIONS

Dragon Day Care • page 88

Lucky House • page 90

12 dragons

Cave Sweet Cave • page 89

1. Door
2. Rhoda
3. Aging
4. Go-go
5. Oven
6. Need
7. Doe
8. Even
9. New

DRAGON DEN

Dragon Worship • page 91

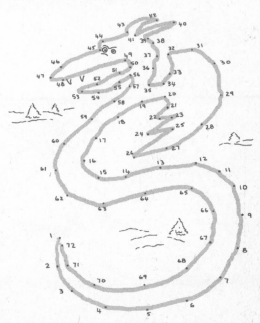

PUZZLE SOLUTIONS

Boulder Dinner • page 92

HOUSE

MOUNTAIN

MOUNTIE

COUCH

FOUNTAIN

SCOUT

MOUSE

Dragons 101 • page 93

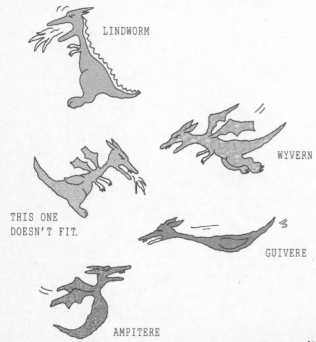

LINDWORM

WYVERN

THIS ONE
DOESN'T FIT.

GUIVERE

AMPITERE

Decorating Dragon • page 94

There are
25 leaves
on the
lamp.

Cave Confusion • page 94

PUZZLE SOLUTIONS

Monster Mash • page 95

Mermaid Mash

Dinner Daydream • page 96

Quarter Question • page 98

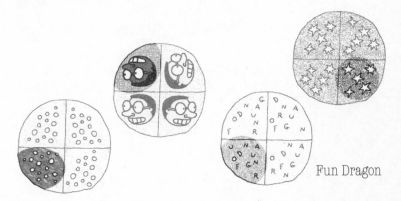

Fun Dragon

PUZZLE SOLUTIONS

Dragon Gate • page 100

Some of the words you can find in
DRAGON GATE are:

great	gear
groan	done
trade	dare
ragged	rate
near	rated
gone	tone
drag	tore
rang	toad
tread	rage
gang	raged
read	tagged
grade	aged
grate	grand
date	nagged
dean	rent
neat	rant
range	

Naughty Dragons • page 101

voracious = hungry
omnivorous = eats many kinds of foods
fantastical = bizarre
serpentine = twisting
malevolent = wicked

Giant Words • page 102

enormous
gigantic
massive
gargantuan
colossal
immense

Ra Ra Ra! • page 102

TRACK

CRACKER

GRASS

CRAB

PIRATE

CRATE

PUZZLE SOLUTIONS

Dragon Discussion • page 103

Gone to get garbage bags

Gruesome Dragsome • page 104

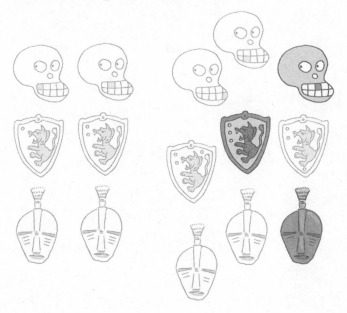

Precious Plunder • page 105

Dragon Tricks • page 106

sMoke
fIre
talons
roar   MICE
claws
magiC
spElls

Fierce Fake • page 107

Hats Off • page 108

CHAPTER 10: DOT-TO-DOT DRAGONS

Big Baby • page 110

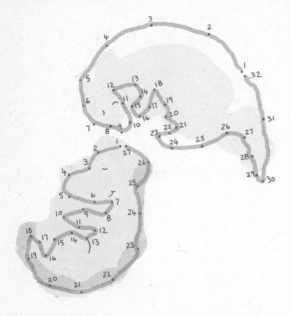

Egg-citing • page 111

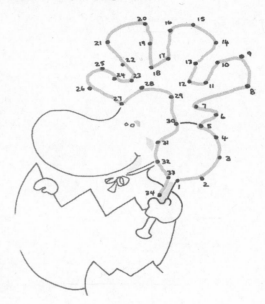

Bigfoot! • page 112

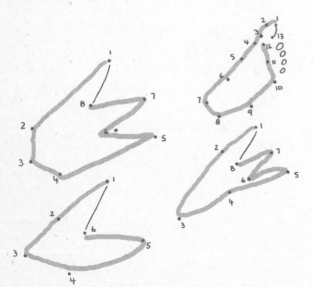

Sharpen Up! • page 113